First Edition
Published by Pendelhaven 2022
121 Place Bourbonniere
Lachute, Quebec
J8H 3W7 Canada

www.pendelhaven.com

ARTIST

Jonathan Burello

AUTHORS

Andy Pfrenger
Andrew Valkauskas

PRODUCER & LAYOUT

Andrew Valkauskas

PROOFING

Sofia De Moura
Aidas Jokubauskas

ISBN: 978-1-988051-28-4

WHEN KING HARALD FAIR-HAIR ESTABLISHED SOLE RULE OVER NORWAY, MANY OF THE LAND'S GREATEST MEN AND WOMEN SET SAIL FOR ICELAND.
THIS IS THE STORY OF THOSE WHO SETTLED ON THE SNAEFELLSNES PENINSULA - EYRBYGGJA SAGA!
THOROLF MOSTUR-BEARD, THE FIRST GREAT SETTLER OF THORSNESS IN NORTHERN SNAEFELLNESS.
HE LOBBED THE HIGH SEAT PILLARS INTO THE SEA... VOWING TO SETTLE WHERE E'ER THEY WASHED ASHORE.
IT WAS A MAGNIFICENT LAND.
WITH LIT TORCH, THOROLF MOSTUR-BEARD RAN THE BREADTH OF THE LAND. EVERYTHING HIS FOOT TOUCHED, WOULD BE HIS DOMINION.
MATERIALS WERE SPARSE.

THOROLF BUILT A TEMPLE TO HONOR THE GODS.
LET NO MAN LOOK UPON THIS HOLY MOUNTAIN WITHOUT FIRST HAVING WASHED.
LET NO CREATURE, NEITHER MAN NOR BEAST, BE HARMED HERE.
LET NO ONE DEFILE THIS SACRED SPACE, EITHER WITH BLOODSHED OR EXCREMENT. THERE IS A ROCK OUT IN THE SEA WHERE YOU CAN DO YOUR BUSINESS.
WAIT. WE GOTTA GO ALL THE WAY OUT THERE TO DROP MUD?

WHEN THE REST OF NORWAY HEARD THAT THERE WAS PLENTY OF LAND AND RESOURCES FOR ALL IN ICELAND, MANY GREAT MEN AND WOMEN SET SAIL FOR THE LAND OF EYR. SETTLERS BEGAN TO ARRIVE IN DROVES.
WELCOME TO ICELAND, MY SON AND BJORN THE EASTERNER. MAY OUR DESCENDANTS PROSPER TOGETHER IN THIS LAND!
THOSE WHO CAME FIRST GOT THE CHOICEST PARCELS OF LAND. THOSE WHO CAME LATER HAD TO SETTLE FOR WHAT WAS LEFT.
A LITTLE TO THE LEFT.
PERFECT.

AROUND THIS TIME, A GREAT VIKING, ARRIVED. HIS NAME WAS THOROLF, THE SON OF GEIRRID. HE THOUGHT HIS MOTHER'S LANDS WERE TOO SMALL.
PATHETIC.
SO HE CHALLENGED ULFAR THE CHAMPION TO A DUEL FOR THE LAND HE OWNED.
I CHALLENGE YOU TO A HOLMGANGR, ULFAR. YOU WILL HAVE TO FIGHT TO KEEP THOSE VERDANT LANDS.
I WILL GUT YOU AND SEND YOUR LIMBS BACK TO YOUR MOTHER!
ULFAR CHOSE TO DIE WITH HONOR RATHER THAN BE BULL ED BY THOROLF.
AND HE DID. BUT THOROLF WAS WOUNDED IN THE LEG. HE WALKED WITH A LIMP FOR THE REST OF HIS LIFE AND GOT HIMSELF THE NICKNAME TWIST-FOOT. VICTORIOUS, THOROLF PROUDLY CLAIMED ULFAR'S PROPERTY.
WHATEVER.

AFTER SOME TIME, THOROLF MOSTUR-BEARD AND BJORN THE EASTERNER PASSED. AWAY.
THE THORSNESSINGS
THE KJALLAKLINGS
AS THE KJALLAKLING CLAN GREW AND GREW, THEY SOON OUTNUMBERED THE THORSNESSINGS. THAT'S WHEN THE TROUBLE STARTED.
WE WILL NO LONGER TOLERATE THE ARROGANCE OF THE THORSNESSINGS!
YOUR FATHER'S DEAD, THORSTEIN COD-BITER. WE'RE DONE TREKKING OUT TO POOP ROCK!
BUT THORSTEIN COD-BITER HAD NO INTENTION OF LETTING THE KJALLAKLINGS DESECRATE THE LAND HIS FATHER HELD SACRED.
THINGS GOT UGLY.
FRIENDS ON BOTH SIDES SENT FOR THORD GELLIR TO HELP SETTLE THE FEUD.
YOU HAVE TO DO SOMETHING. YOU'RE A KINSMAN OF THE KJALLAKLINGS.
AND YOUR SISTER IS MARRIED TO THORSTEIN COD-BITER.
NO COMPENSATION WILL BE PAID FOR THE LIVES. THIS LAND IS NO LONGER SACRED DUE TO THE BLOOD SPILLED HERE.
WE WILL MOVE THE ASSEMBLY TO THE WESTERN SIDE OF THE HEADLAND. YOU CAN GO TO THE BATHROOM WHEREVER YOU WANT HERE.

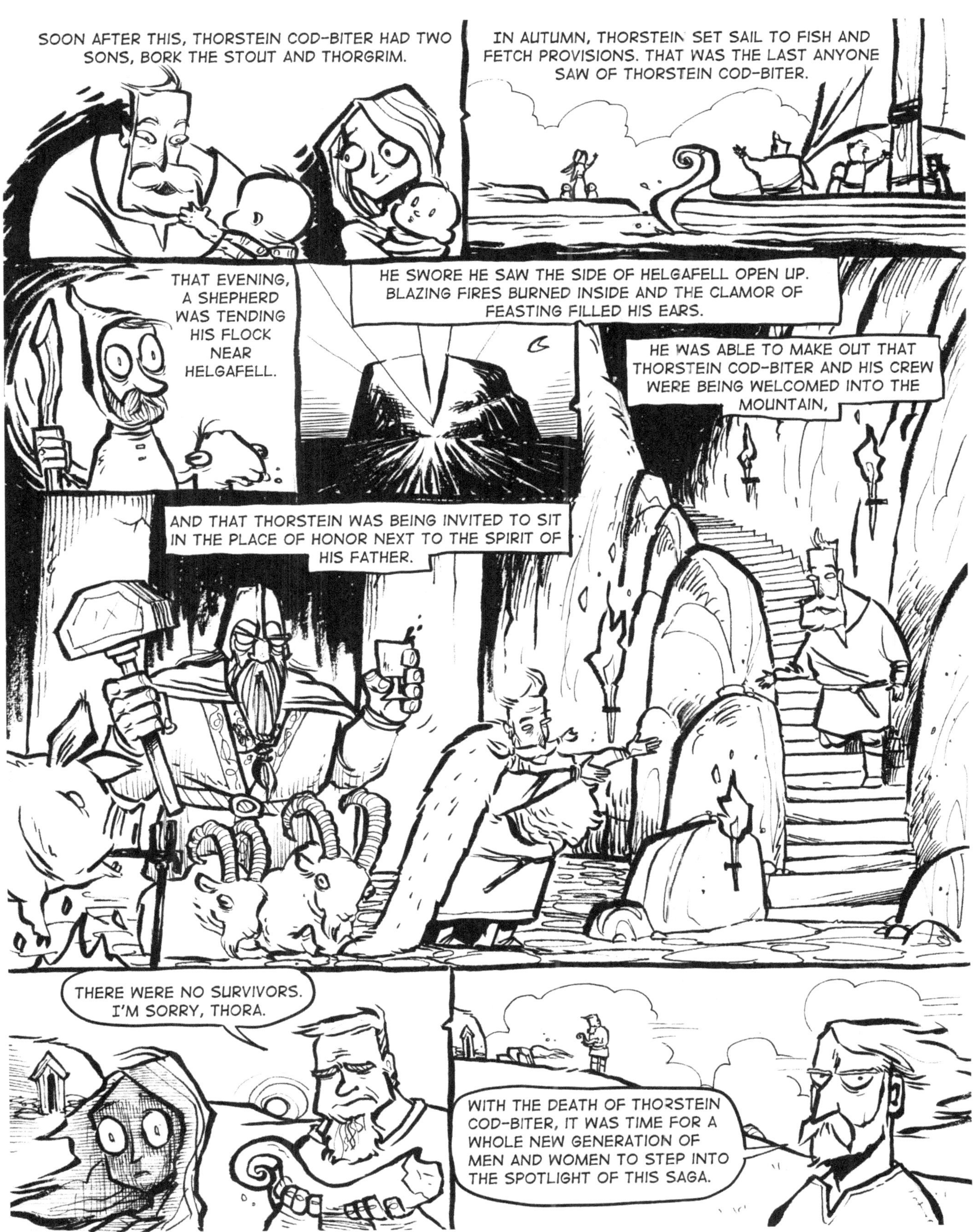
SOON AFTER THIS, THORSTEIN COD-BITER HAD TWO SONS, BORK THE STOUT AND THORGRIM.
IN AUTUMN, THORSTEIN SET SAIL TO FISH AND FETCH PROVISIONS. THAT WAS THE LAST ANYONE SAW OF THORSTEIN COD-BITER.
THAT EVENING, A SHEPHERD WAS TENDING HIS FLOCK NEAR HELGAFELL.
HE SWORE HE SAW THE SIDE OF HELGAFELL OPEN UP. BLAZING FIRES BURNED INSIDE AND THE CLAMOR OF FEASTING FILLED HIS EARS.
HE WAS ABLE TO MAKE OUT THAT THORSTEIN COD-BITER AND HIS CREW WERE BEING WELCOMED INTO THE MOUNTAIN,
AND THAT THORSTEIN WAS BEING INVITED TO SIT IN THE PLACE OF HONOR NEXT TO THE SPIRIT OF HIS FATHER.
THERE WERE NO SURVIVORS. I'M SORRY, THORA.
WITH THE DEATH OF THORSTEIN COD-BITER, IT WAS TIME FOR A WHOLE NEW GENERATION OF MEN AND WOMEN TO STEP INTO THE SPOTLIGHT OF THIS SAGA.

THE MOST IMPORTANT OF THEM WAS THORSTEIN COD-BITER'S GRANDSON. HE HAD A ROUGH START IN LIFE.
BEFORE HE WAS BORN, HIS FATHER, THORGRIM, WAS KILLED IN A NASTY FEUD WITH GISLI SURSSON. BUT THAT'S A WHOLE OTHER SAGA.
SOON AFTER, HIS SON THORGRIM JR WAS BORN.
HIS MOTHER MOVED BACK TO HELGAFELL AND MARRIED BORK THE STOUT.
BUT YOUNG THORGRIM WAS SENT TO ALFTAFJORD TO BE FOSTERED BY THORBRAND.
HE WAS A DIFFICULT CHILD, SO THEY CALLED HIM SNORRI (THAT MEANS "SHARP-WITTED," BUT SOME PEOPLE WILL TELL YOU IT MEANS "WARLIKE.")
TIME PASSED QUICKLY. AND WHEN SNORRI WAS 14, HE TRAVELED TO NORWAY WITH HIS FOSTER-BROTHERS THORLEIF KIMBI AND THORODD. HIS UNCLE BORK EVEN PAID FOR THE TRIP.
B

SNORRI AND THE THORBRANDSSONS CAME HOME JUST BEFORE WINTER. THORLEIF AND THORODD HAD NEW HORSES AND FINE CLOTHES. SNORRI DID NOT.
WHEN SNORRI ARRIVED AT HELGAFELL, EVERYONE MADE FUN OF HIS OUTFIT.
LOOKS LIKE SNORRI LOST ALL HIS MONEY.
WHAT AN OLD NAG.
I GAVE YOU 50 PIECES OF SILVER. WHERE DID IT GO?
I DEMAND YOU GIVE ME MY INHERITANCE FROM MY FATHER.
YOU SEEM LIKE A MAN WHO'S DOWN ON HIS LUCK, SNORRI. LET'S NOT SHARE HELGAFELL. WHY DON'T I PAY YOU FOR YOUR HALF. LEAST I CAN DO.
WHY DON'T YOU SET A PRICE ON THE PLACE AND LEAVE ME TO DECIDE IF I CAN PAY OR NOT?
60 PIECES OF SILVER.
DEAL! THORBRAND, THE BAG.
B
BORK. UNRELATED NOTE. I'M LEAVING YOU.
SNORRI'S SHREWD MIND EARNED HIM A LOT OF RESPECT IN THE DISTRICT. BEFORE LONG, HE BECAME A CHIEFTAIN AND TEMPLE PRIEST LIKE HIS GREAT-GRANDFATHER, THOROLF MOSTUR-BEARD.
PEOPLE CALLED HIM SNORRI GOðI.

WHILE SNORRI WAS GAINING A REPUTATION, A FEUD WAS BREWING NEARBY BETWEEN GEIRRID, THE DAUGHTER OF THOROLF TWIST-FOOT, AND A WITCH CALLED KATLA OVER SNORRI'S NEPHEW.
SNORRI'S SISTER, THURID, MARRIED THORBJORN THE STOUT. THEY HAD THREE SONS. GUNNLAUG WAS ONE.
GUNNLAUG LIKED TO HANG OUT WITH A BOY NAMED ODD. HE WAS THE SON OF KATLA.
SHE WAS NOT VERY POPULAR.
GUNNLAUG ALSO LIKED TO SPEND TIME AT MAVAHLID WITH GEIRRID, THOROLF TWIST-FOOT'S DAUGHTER.
ZZZZ
BECAUSE SHE KNEW A THING OR TWO ABOUT A THING OR TWO.
OFF TO SEE THAT OLD HAG GEIRRID AGAIN, GUNNLAUG??
YOU'RE NOT SO YOUNG YOURSELF, KATLA.
SHE'S NOT THE ONLY WOMAN WITH THOUGHTS IN HER HEAD.

YOU SHOULD STAY HERE TONIGHT, GUNNLAUG. THERE ARE SEA SPIRITS ABOUT AND YOU DON'T LOOK LIKE A LUCKY MAN.
WE'LL BE FINE.
INVITE GUNNLAUG TO STAY THE NIGHT, ODD.
HE'S ALREADY ON HIS WAY HOME.
THEN LET HIM FACE WHAT'S COMING TO HIM.
LATE THAT NIGHT, THORBJORN STEPPED OUTSIDE TO LOOK FOR HIS SON.
GUNNLAUG!
HE FOUND HIM.
GUNNLAUG SPENT THE WHOLE WINTER RECOVERING. ALL THE WHILE, PEOPLE TALKED.
I HEARD IT WAS THAT OLD WITCH, GEIRRID. BET SHE RODE HIM ALL OVER THE COUNTRYSIDE.
THORBJORN RODE TO MAVAHLID TO BRING A CASE AGAINST GEIRR'D. SNORRI WAS THERE TO SUPPORT HIS BROTHER-IN-LAW.
YOU WITCHED UP MY SON! WE'LL SEE YOU IN COURT.
THE CASE WAS HEARD AT THE THORSNESS ASSEMBLY. SNORRI THOUGHT HE HAD IT WRAPPED UP BUT HE DIDN'T COUNT ON ARNKEL (GEIRRID'S BROTHER) AND THORARIN THE BLACK TO DEFEND HER.
WE SWEAR GEIRRID DID NO HARM.
THIS WAS THE FIRST TIME SNORRI LOST TO ARNKEL. IT WOULDN'T BE THE LAST.
WE DECLARE GEIRRID INNOCENT!

GEIRRID'S SON, THORARIN THE BLACK, HAD A PRIZED FIGHTING STALLION THAT HE KEPT UP IN THE MOUNTAINS.
I WISH YOU WERE AS BOLD AS THAT HORSE, THORARIN.
THAT SUMMER, THORBJORN THE STOUT LEFT A HERD OF STUD HORSES TO GRAZE IN THE MOUNTAINS NEAR THORARIN'S STALLION.
IN AUTUMN, THORBJORN'S HORSES WENT MISSING.
IT MUST HAVE BEEN THORARIN THE BLACK GETTING REVENGE FOR WHAT HAPPENED TO HIS MOTHER LAST YEAR.
THORBJORN SET OUT AT ONCE.
WE'VE COME TO SEARCH YOUR PROPERTY FOR MY STOLEN HORSES!
DO YOU HAVE A... WARRANT?
WHAT ARE YOU GONNA DO ABOUT IT?
RIGHT-O. GO AHEAD.

HOW CAN YOU BE THOROLF TWIST-FOOT'S GRANDSON?
STOP!!
THAT'S MY BOY.
YOU'LL BE HEARING FROM MY LAWYER!
SOMEBODY LOSE A HAND?
AUD.
IT'S NOTHING.

THORARIN FINALLY PROVED HE WAS A MAN TODAY, BUT WHAT WILL PEOPLE SAY WHEN THEY FIND OUT HE CHOPPED OFF THE HAND OF HIS OWN WIFE!
SLICE
"THORBJORN'S CORPSE WILL FEED THE EAGLES, BUT ODD GOT AWAY.
SNORRI GOÐI ISN'T GOING TO LIKE THIS. WE'RE GONNA NEED SOME HELP.
EXPECTING THE WORST FROM SNORRI, THORARIN RIDES OUT TO VISIT HIS BROTHER-IN-LAW, VERMUND THE SLENDER, A SON OF THORGRIM KJALLAKSSON AND AN INFLUENTIAL FIGURE IN THE REGION.
WE NEED YOUR UNCLE ARNKEL.
STAY WITH ME FOR THE WINTER. I'LL HANDLE SNORRI GOÐI.

MEANWHILE, BACK AT MAVAHLID, GEIRRID LEARNED SOME VALUABLE INFORMATION.
ODD KATLASSON CUT MY HAND OFF.
HMMM.
GEIRRID SPREAD THE NEWS AND SOON THORARIN AND ARNKEL WERE ON THEIR WAY TO SETTLE THE ISSUE. BUT KATLA KNEW THEY WERE COMING AND SHE HAD A FEW TRICKS UP HER SLEEVE.
ODD'S NOT HERE.
WE'LL SEARCH ANYWAY.
WOW. NOTHING
DID THAT GOAT SEEM UNUSUAL TO YOU.
I THOUGHT THIS MIGHT HAPPEN.
BACK AGAIN SO SOON?
AND THIS IS HOW THE FEUD BETWEEN GEIRRID AND KATLA ENDED.
YOUR WICKED MOTHER BROUGHT YOU TO THIS END, ODD.

I MAY BE WICKED, BUT THIS IS TOO FAR! I ADMIT THAT I CAUSED GUNNLAUG'S ACCIDENT. I CAUSED THE TROUBLE. BUT I'LL NEVER FORGIVE YOU FOR THIS. AND I CURSE YOU ARNKEL! YOU'LL SUFFER MORE PAIN FROM YOUR FATHER THAN I EVER CAUSED ODD. SOON ALL WILL SEE WHAT AN EVIL MAN THOROLF TWIST-FOOT IS!
NO ONE WAS SORRY TO HEAR THAT KATLA AND ODD HAD MET THEIR END. BUT THAT'S NOT THE END OF OUR STORY.
SNORRI GOÐI TRIED TO BRING A LAWSUIT AGAINST THORBJORN'S KILLERS...AND KATLA'S AND ODD'S TOO. VERMUND SWORE TO SUPPORT THORARIN.
ARNKEL PAID FOR THE TWO MEN TO TRAVEL ABROAD. WHEN SNORRI HEARD ABOUT THE PLAN, HE BURNED THE SHIP.
BUT ARNKEL HAD PREPARED ANOTHER BOAT, JUST IN CASE.
SNORRI BROUGHT HIS CASE TO THE THORSNESS ASSEMBLY AND WON.
THORARIN IS SENTENCED TO OUTLAWRY. SNORRI GOÐI WILL TAKE CONTROL OF HIS PROPERTY.
HELP ME OUT HERE AND I PROMISE TO HAVE YOUR BACK WHENEVER YOU NEED ME.
THIS WAS THE FIRST OF MANY VICTORIES FOR YOUNG SNORRI.

LATER THAT FALL, THORBJORN'S MISSING HERD OF HORSES WAS FOUND UP IN THE MOUNTAINS. THEY WERE ALL DEAD. IT TURNS OUT THAT THORARIN'S STALLION DROVE THEM INTO A PASS WHERE THEY WERE SNOWED IN AND KILLED.
AFTER THORBJORN'S DEATH, RUMORS STARTED TO CIRCULATE ABOUT THURID RECEIVING VISITS AT FRODRIVER FROM A MAN CALLED BJORN.
WHEN SNORRI HEARD ABOUT IT, HE "INVITED" HIS SISTER TO COME STAY WITH HIM.
NOT LONG AFTER, SNORRI MARRIED THURID TO A WEALTHY MERCHANT CALLED THORODD TRIBUTE-TRADER. AND YES, IT WAS ABOUT THE MONEY.
MEANWHILE, VERMUND THE SLENDER WAS WAITING OUT HIS TERM OF EXILE BY SERVING AS A RETAINER FOR EARL HAKON SIGURDARSON.

YOU'RE A REMARKABLE MAN, VERMUND.
THESE BERZERKERS WERE A GIFT FROM KING EIRIK OF SWEDEN. HALLI AND LEIKNIR. THEY'RE USEFUL MEN, AS LONG AS THEY'RE NOT ANGRY.
IN SPRING, VERMUND TOLD THE EARL THAT HE WAS PREPARED TO RETURN TO ICELAND.
YOU ARE ALWAYS FREE TO GO. PLEASE, CHOOSE A GIFT THAT WILL BRING YOU BOTH PRESTIGE AND HONOR AT HOME.
SHOVE
I'LL TAKE THE BERSERKER BROTHERS!
ARE YOU SURE ABOUT THAT?
YOU'RE GOING TO LOVE ICELAND, BOYS.
ARE THERE WOMEN?
THEY GOT SETTLED.
BUT THEY GOT RESTLESS REAL QUICK.
YOU SAID YOU'D TAKE CARE OF US. I WANT A WOMAN.
HE WANT WOMAN.

WHEN VERMUND DIDN'T DELIVER, THINGS GOT UGLY.
HE WANT WOMAN!
IN AUTUMN, VERMUND HELD A FEAST. HE INVITED HIS BROTHER, KILLER-STYR AND ARNKEL.
WOULD YOU LIKE A PAIR OF BERSERKERS? HARDLY USED.
GIVE THEM TO KILLER-STYR. THEY'RE A GREAT MATCH.
YOU ARE SUCH A GREAT BROTHER. I 'D LIKE TO PRESENT THESE BERSERKERS TO YOU AS A GIFT.
STYR KNEW THEY'D BE TROUBLE BUT ACCEPTED THE "GIFT."
THE BERSERKERS WEREN'T TOO HAPPY BEING PASSED AROUND LIKE PROPERTY.
WOMAN?
THE BROTHERS ENJOYED LIFE WITH KILLER-STYR MUCH BETTER.
BUT THINGS STARTED HEADING SOUTH WHEN HALLI TOOK AN INTEREST IN STYR'S DAUGHTER, ASDIS.

GO AHEAD. YOU CAN TOUCH MY BICEP.

UM...OK?

DON'T YOU DARE TRY TO SEDUCE MY DAUGHTER, HALLI!

I LOVE HER!

I DON'T WANT TROUBLE, STYR

I'M NOT SAYING NO. JUST GIVE ME A FEW DAYS TO THINK IT OVER.

THE FOLLOWING MORNING, STYR WENT TO SEE SNORRI GOðI FOR SOME MUCH NEEDED ADVICE.

HERE'S WHAT YOU SHOULD DO...

I WILL LET YOU MARRY ASDIS, BUT FIRST YOU MUST COMPLETE A FEW DIFFICULT TASKS TO PROVE YOU ARE WORTHY.

FIRST, YOU NEED TO CLEAR A PATH THROUGH THIS LAVA FIELD ALL THE WAY TO BJORN'S HAVEN.

WHEN THEY FINISHED THE WORK, STYR INVITED THE TWO BROTHERS INTO HIS NEWLY BUILT BATHHOUSE.
THUMP
HEY! THAT'S TOO MUCH STEAM, STYR!
gasp *gasp* *gasp*
STAB STAB STAB
Pant pant pant
!
SPEAKING OF MARRIAGE...
IN AUTUMN, ASDIS MARRIED SNORRI GOðI. EVERYONE SAID IT WAS A GOOD MATCH, ESPECIALLY FOR SNORRI AND STYR.
AROUND THIS TIME, SNORRI GOT NEWS THAT THURID WAS ONCE AGAIN RECEIVING VISITS FROM BJORN THE BREIDAVIK CHAMPION.

BE CAREFUL ON YOUR WAY HOME, BJORN. I THINK THORODD MAY TRY TO PUT AN END TO YOUR VISITS.
trot trot trot
THE AMBUSH DIDN'T GO AS PLANNED.
BUT THORODD WASN'T DONE WITH BJORN.
YOU'LL NEVER BELIEVE IT. BJORN KILLED THORIR'S SONS! HE HAS TO PAY!
I GOT THIS.
AND SNORRI DID. HE TOOK THE CASE AND CONVICTED BJORN WITH A SENTENCE OF MINOR OUTLAWRY. THAT'S THREE YEARS OF EXILE FROM ICELAND.
BJORN SPENT HIS EXILE WITH THE JOMSVIKINGS, A FAMOUS BAND OF VIKINGS. HE FOUGHT BRAVELY ALONGSIDE PALNA-TOKI AND STYRNBJORN THE STRONG.
THAT SUMMER, THURID GAVE BIRTH TO A HANDSOME BABY BOY. SHE NAMED HIM KJARTAN.

THIS NEXT STORY BEGINS WITH A DISPUTE BETWEEN THOROLF TWIST-FOOT AND A FREEDMAN NAMED ULFAR.
THEY SHARED OWNERSHIP OF THE HILLTOP MEADOW.
HURRY, BOYS. RAIN IS COMING!
"IT'LL CLEAR. LET'S MOW THE HOME MEADOW TODAY. WE'LL TEND TO THE HILL MEADOW TOMORROW.
STILL EXPECTING RAIN, THOROLF WORKED THEIR SHARED MEADOW ON THE HILL.
TAKE ULFAR'S HAY TOO.
The next morning...
!
IT WASN'T A FIGHT ULFAR COULD WIN ALONE. SO HE ASKED THOROLF'S SON, ARNKEL, FOR HELP.
COULDN'T YOU JUST PAY ULFAR FOR THE HAY YOU TOOK? FOR ME?
NO.
SORRY ABOUT MY FATHER. I'LL COVER IT MYSELF.
YOU'RE A POWERFUL MAN, RIGHT? HE SHOULD DO WHAT *YOU* SAY.
I NEED YOU PAY ME BACK FOR THAT HAY NOW.
NOT HAPPENING.

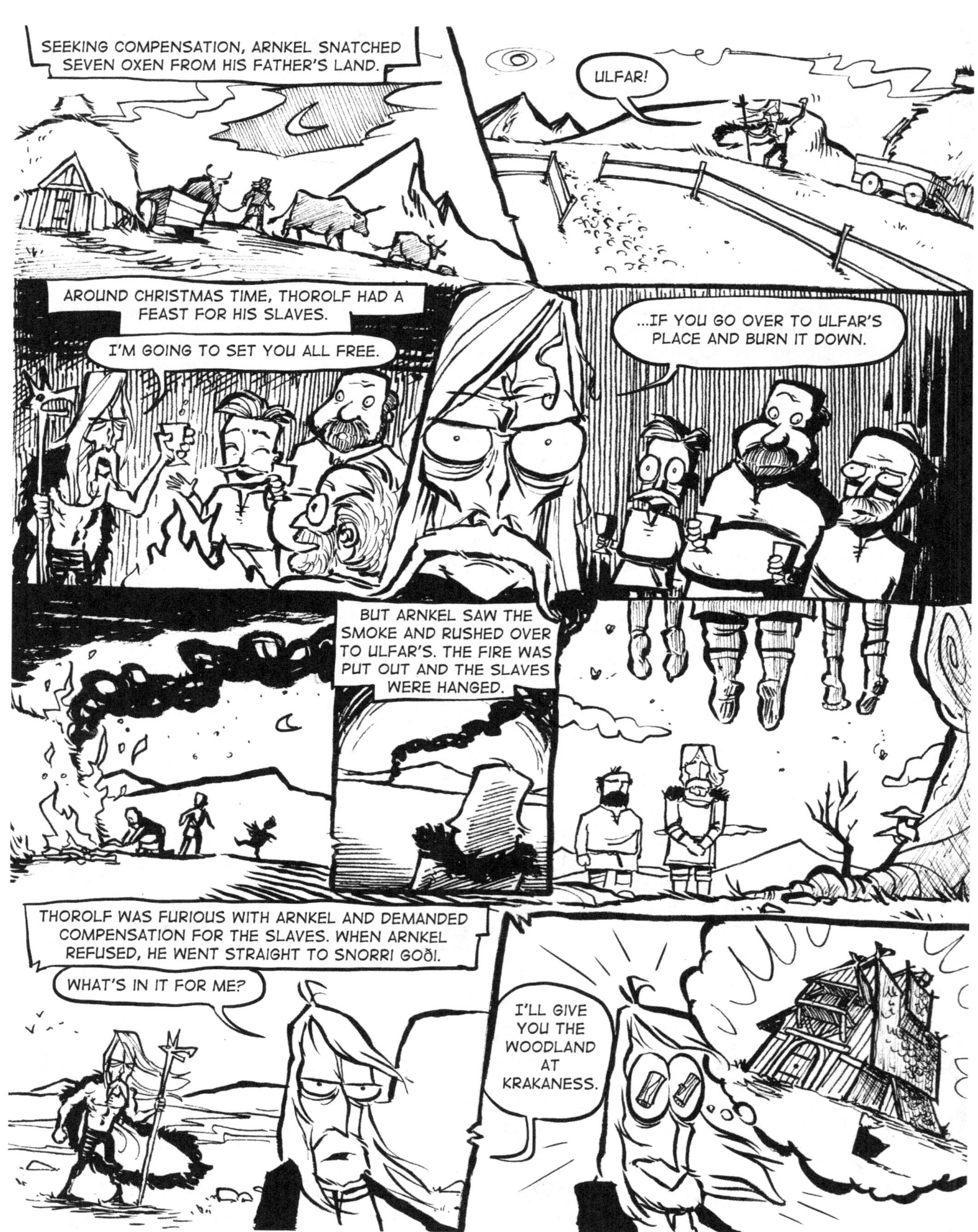
SEEKING COMPENSATION, ARNKEL SNATCHED SEVEN OXEN FROM HIS FATHER'S LAND.
ULFAR!
AROUND CHRISTMAS TIME, THOROLF HAD A FEAST FOR HIS SLAVES.
I'M GOING TO SET YOU ALL FREE.
...IF YOU GO OVER TO ULFAR'S PLACE AND BURN IT DOWN.
BUT ARNKEL SAW THE SMOKE AND RUSHED OVER TO ULFAR'S. THE FIRE WAS PUT OUT AND THE SLAVES WERE HANGED.
THOROLF WAS FURIOUS WITH ARNKEL AND DEMANDED COMPENSATION FOR THE SLAVES. WHEN ARNKEL REFUSED, HE WENT STRAIGHT TO SNORRI GOÐI.
WHAT'S IN IT FOR ME?
I'LL GIVE YOU THE WOODLAND AT KRAKANESS.

SNORRI TOOK THE CASE. AND HE WON, BUT JUST BARELY. THOROLF WASN'T HAPPY WITH THE AMOUNT HE WAS PAID EITHER.
I AM HANDING MY PROPERTY OVER TO YOU AS ITS GUARDIAN, ARNKEL.
THIS ARRANGEMENT DIDN'T PLEASE SNORRI'S FOSTER-BROTHERS, THE THORBRANDSSONS.
AND WHEN ULFAR'S BROTHER DIED, HE AND ARNKEL RACED THE THORBRANDSSONS TO CLAIM HIS PROPERTY TOO.
BUT WE GAVE ULFAR AND HIS BROTHER ORLYG THIS LAND WHEN WE SET THEM FREE. IT'S STILL OURS.
BAAA!
AH AH AH. YOU GAVE THEM PROPERTY. AS HIS REPRESENTATIVE AND NOW HEIR, I SAY THE PROPERTY IS OURS.
THE THORBRANDSSONS WENT TO SNORRI GOÐI FOR HELP.
AS OUR FOSTER BROTHER, YOU'VE GOT TO HELP US.
YOU SHOULD HAVE CLAIMED THE PROPERTY FIRST. THERE'S NOTHING I CAN DO.
THAT AUTUMN, ULFAR WAS INVITED TO A FEAST AT ARNKEL'S HOUSE. HE WAS TREATED WELL AND GIVEN FINE GIFTS AS HE LEFT.
THERE HE IS. YOU KNOW WHAT TO DO.

COOL SWORD, ULFAR. CAN I SEE IT?
!
HA-HA!
GO SEE WHO THAT IS WITH ULFAR'S SWORD AND SHIELD.
RUN AND TELL THE THORBRANDSSONS TO HURRY OVER TO ULFAR'S. THEY SHOULD CLAIM THAT PROPERTY BEFORE MY SON ROBS THEM AGAIN.
ARGH!
IT'S OURS, BOYS.
YOU'D BETTER TURN AROUND, THORLEIF.
AND ONCE AGAIN, THE THORBRANDSSONS WENT TO SNORRI GOÐI FOR HELP.
IT'S IMPOSSIBLE NOW THAT HE'S GOT HIS HANDS ON EVERYTHING. ARNKEL ALWAYS GETS WHAT HE WANTS.
TRUE ENOUGH, FOSTER BROTHER. I KNEW YOU WOULDN'T DEFEND US AGAINST HIM. YOU'VE LOST EVERY FIGHT YOU'VE HAD WITH HIM!

THINGS WERE QUIET FOR A TIME, UNTIL THOROLF TWIST-FOOT TRIED TO CLAIM THE WOODLAND BACK FROM SNORRI GOÐI.
I DIDN'T GIVE IT TO YOU. IT WAS A LOAN!
I DON'T THINK SO.
IF WE COULD STOP FIGHTING, YOU AND I COULD RUN THIS DISTRICT. BUT WE NEED TO DEAL WITH SNORRI FIRST.
YOU WON'T HELP BECAUSE YOU'RE A COWARD!
THINK WHAT YOU WANT. I'M NOT LETTING YOU AND YOUR TERRIBLE NATURE DRAG ME INTO A FIGHT WITH SNORRI.
AND SO, THOROLF WENT HOME AND HE RAGED.
SLAM
AND RAGED.
AND RAGED.
UNTIL HE DIED.
GET ARNKEL.
WE NEED TO LAY HIM DOWN AND CLOSE HIS EYES.

IT WAS CUSTOM THEN NOT TO CARRY A BODY OUT THROUGH THE DOOR, FOR FEAR IT MIGHT COME BACK.
WHY IS HE SO HEAVY?
THIS ISN'T A GOOD SIGN.
AFTER THOROLF DIED, THINGS GOT . . . UNPLEASANT.
!
!
THOROLF'S REIGN OF TERROR LASTED ALL SUMMER, FORCING MANY TO ABANDON THEIR FARMS.
AND THOSE HE KILLED WERE LATER SEEN WALKING BY HIS SIDE AT NIGHT. THIS LASTED ALL WINTER.

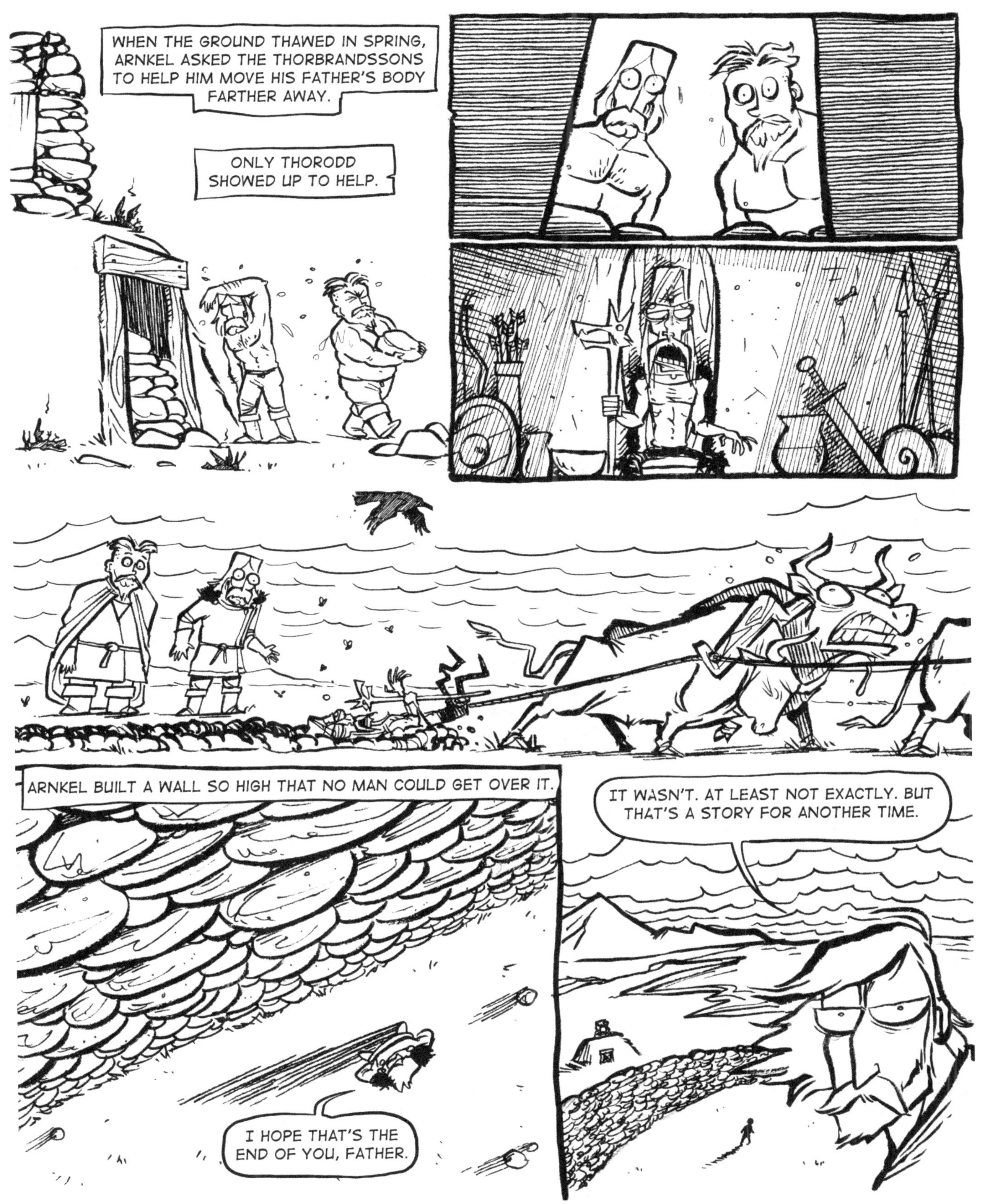
WHEN THE GROUND THAWED IN SPRING, ARNKEL ASKED THE THORBRANDSSONS TO HELP HIM MOVE HIS FATHER'S BODY FARTHER AWAY.
ONLY THORODD SHOWED UP TO HELP.
ARNKEL BUILT A WALL SO HIGH THAT NO MAN COULD GET OVER IT.
I HOPE THAT'S THE END OF YOU, FATHER.
IT WASN'T. AT LEAST NOT EXACTLY. BUT THAT'S A STORY FOR ANOTHER TIME.

WITH THE DEATH OF THOROLF TWIST-FOOT, THERE WAS NOTHING STOPPING SNORRI FROM TAKING FULL ADVANTAGE OF KRAKANESS WOOD.
HE HAS NO RIGHT. THESE WOODS SHOULD HAVE GONE TO ME.
ONE DAY, SNORRI SENT HIS SLAVES TO FETCH SOME OF THE DRIED TIMBER. HIS FRIEND HAUK WENT ALONG TO HELP
HAUK WAS THE FIRST TO SPOT ARNKEL RIDING UP.
THE STREAM CAME TO BE KNOWN AS HAUK'S RIVER AFTER THAT.
IN SPRING, SNORRI BROUGHT A LAWSUIT AGAINST ARNKEL FOR THE KILLING OF HAUK. BUT...
BECAUSE HAUK ATTACKED ARNKEL WITHOUT PROVOCATION, SNORRI'S LAWSUIT IS WITHOUT MERIT.
IN THE FALL, SNORRI WAS APPROACHED BY AN OUTLAW LOOKING FOR A PLACE TO STAY. SNORRI SPOKE TO HIM FOR A LONG WHILE BEFORE SENDING HIM AWAY.

SOON AFTER, THE OUTLAW SHOWED UP AT ARNKEL'S TO ASK FOR WORK.
DIDN'T YOU JUST COME FROM SNORRI'S FARM?
YEAH, BUT I'M NOT INTERESTED IN STAYING WITH SOMEONE WHO IS ALWAYS ON THE LOSING SIDE OF EVERYTHING. I'D PREFER TO STAY WITH YOU.
I DON'T USUALLY TAKE IN MEN FROM OUTSIDE THE DISTRICT.
I'M SORRY. NOTHING I CAN DO FOR YOU.
THWACK
RUMOR SPREAD THAT SNORRI HAD SENT THE OUTLAW. SNORRI LET PEOPLE SAY WHAT THEY WANTED.
A YEAR LATER, SNORRI HOSTED A GREAT FEAST. PEOPLE GOT TO TALKING ABOUT WHO WAS THE BEST MAN IN THE DISTRICT.
ARNKEL'S CLEARLY THE BETTER MAN. HE ALWAYS WINS!
HE'S RIGHT. ARNKEL PAID NOTHING FOR KILLING SNORRI'S FRIEND, HAUK!
AFTER THE FEAST, SNORRI WALKED THE THORBRANDSSONS DOWN TO THEIR SHIP.
I WANT YOU TO HAVE THIS BEAUTIFUL AXE, THORLEIF. THE LONG HANDLE MIGHT COME IN HANDY IF YOU SEE ARNKEL ON YOUR WAY HOME, THOUGH I'M NOT SURE IT'S LONG ENOUGH TO REACH HIS HEAD.
YOU TELL ME WHEN YOU'RE READY TO AVENGE HAUK. I WON'T BE SLOW TO SWING THIS AXE BY YOUR SIDE.

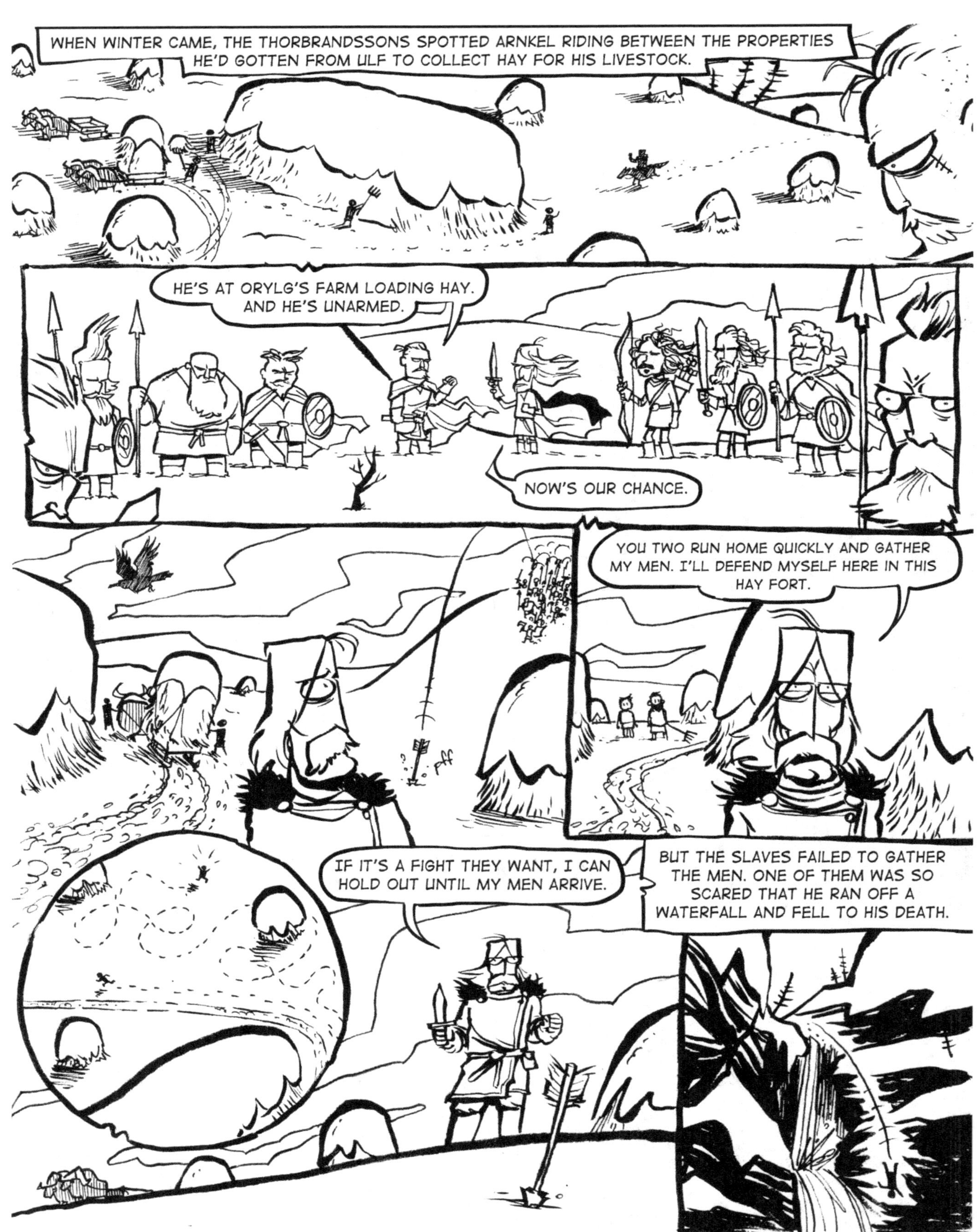
WHEN WINTER CAME, THE THORBRANDSSONS SPOTTED ARNKEL RIDING BETWEEN THE PROPERTIES HE'D GOTTEN FROM ULF TO COLLECT HAY FOR HIS LIVESTOCK.
HE'S AT ORYLG'S FARM LOADING HAY. AND HE'S UNARMED.
NOW'S OUR CHANCE.
pff
YOU TWO RUN HOME QUICKLY AND GATHER MY MEN. I'LL DEFEND MYSELF HERE IN THIS HAY FORT.
IF IT'S A FIGHT THEY WANT, I CAN HOLD OUT UNTIL MY MEN ARRIVE.
BUT THE SLAVES FAILED TO GATHER THE MEN. ONE OF THEM WAS SO SCARED THAT HE RAN OFF A WATERFALL AND FELL TO HIS DEATH.

THE OTHER MADE IT HOME, BUT THE FOOL GOT DISTRACTED.
GUYS!
HEY, CAN YOU GIVE US A HAND WITH THIS?
OH, SURE.

BACK AT ARNKEL'S FARM, THE SLAVES HAD FINISHED UNLOADING THE HAY.
WHERE'S ARNKEL?
THEY BURIED ARNKEL BY THE SEA AND RAISED A MOUND OVER HIS GRAVE AS LARGE AS A HAYSTACK.
ARNKEL WAS THE MOST GIFTED, INTELLIGENT, KIND-HEARTED MAN.
THE BRAVEST.
THE MOST HONEST.
ALWAYS GOOD-TEMPERED.
ARNKEL'S MOTHER, GEIRRID, TRIED TO BRING A SUIT AGAINST SNORRI FOR THE KILLING, BUT SHE HANDLED IT POORLY. IT WAS ANOTHER VICTORY FOR SNORRI.
?
?
?
FOR LANDING THE KILLING BLOW, THORLEIF KIMBI WAS ONLY SENTENCED TO MINOR OUTLAWRY.
SEE YOU IN THREE YEARS, FOSTER-BROTHER!
EVERYONE THOUGHT THIS WAS A TERRIBLE OUTCOME AND A SHAME TO ARNKEL'S MEMORY.

THORLEIF KIMBI PREPARED FOR HIS SENTENCE OF OUTLAWRY BY BOOKING PASSAGE ON A TRADING VESSEL. AS THEY PREPARED TO LEAVE, A STRANGER APPROACHED.
MY NAME IS ARNBJORN ASBRANDSSON OF KAMB. I NEED TO GET TO DENMARK TO LOOK FOR MY BROTHER BJORN.
AND SO, THE SHIP LEFT ICELAND WITH BOTH THORLEIF KIMBI AND ARNBJORN ABOARD.
WHEN THEY LANDED IN HORDALAND, IT WAS THORLEIF'S TURN TO DO THE COOKING FOR THE CREW. BUT ARNBJORN HAD GOTTEN TO SHORE WITH THE PORRIDGE POT BEFORE HIM.
HURRY UP THORLEIF. WE'RE HUNGRY!
WHY IS EVERYONE FROM ICELAND SO SLOW?
GIVE ME THAT POT, ARNBJORN. I NEED TO COOK PORRIDGE FOR THE CREW NOW.
MY FOOD ISN'T READY YET.
KICK!
IT'S DONE NOW.

WAP!
AS THE ONLY ICELANDERS HERE, WE SHOULDN'T FIGHT IN FRONT OF THESE NORWEGIANS. BUT I WON'T FORGET THIS WHEN WE MEET AGAIN IN ICELAND.
THE TWO MEN PARTED WAYS SHORTLY AFTER. THORLEIF SPENT HIS EXILE IN NORWAY AND THEN RETURNED TO ICELAND. ARNBJORN TRAVELED TO DENMARK AND FOUND HIS BROTHER BJORN. THEY ALL RETURNED TO ICELAND A FEW YEARS LATER.
ONE DAY A LARGE CROWD GATHERED NEAR FROD RIVER TO TRADE. THURID WAS THERE WITH THORODD AND THE CHILD, KJARTAN. BJORN WAS THERE TOO.
LATER, BJORN RODE HOME WITH HIS BROTHER AND THORD THORLAKSSON.
DID YOU NOTICE YOUNG KJARTAN, THE SON OF THURID AND . . . SOMEONE ELSE?
I SAW HIM, THORD.
I SUGGEST YOU TRY TO FORGET THURID.
MY HEAD SAYS YOU'RE RIGHT, BUT MY HEART SAYS OTHERWISE, FRIEND.
GOOD LUCK DEALING WITH HER BROTHER SNORRI.
BJORN FOLLOWED HIS HEART.
FEELING HOPELESS, THORODD PAID A VISIT TO WIFE OF THORIR WOOD-LEG, THORGRIMA WITCH-FACE.
YOU GOTTA HELP ME!

AFTER THREE DAYS OF SHELTERING IN A CAVE, AN EXHAUSTED BJORN MADE HIS WAY HOME.
BJORN STAYED HOME AT KAMB FOR THE REST OF THAT WINTER.
IN THE SPRING, THORLEIF KIMBI APPROACHED THE THORLAKSSONS TO ASK FOR THEIR SISTER'S HAND IN MARRIAGE.
I THINK IT'S A GREAT IDEA, THORD!
YOU CAN MARRY MY SISTER WHEN THE SCARS ON YOUR NECK HEAL FROM THAT PORRIDGE IN NORWAY THREE YEARS AGO.
I'M NOT SURE I'LL GET MY REVENGE ANYTIME SOON, BUT I BET I CAN KNOCK YOU AROUND WITHIN THE NEXT THREE YEARS.
YOU DON'T SCARE ME, THORLEIF.
THE NEXT MORNING THE THORLAKSSONS WALKED BY AS THE THORBRANDSSONS WERE PLAYING A TURF GAME.
SPLAT!
A SQUABBLE ENSUED.
WHEN THE DUST SETTLED, SNORRI GOÐI AND STEINTHOR THORLAKSSON ARRANGED A SETTLEMENT.
BOTH SIDES WENT HOME AND THE MATTER APPEARED TO BE SETTLED. BUT IT WASN'T.

THAT SUMMER, THE THORBRANDSSONS TRIED TO GET THEIR REVENGE ON ARNBJORN.
CLEAR OFF OF THERE! AND STOP CAUSING TROUBLE, FOSTER BROTHERS.
THE THORBRANDSSONS OBEYED SNORRI, BUT THEY WEREN'T HAPPY ABOUT IT.
NOT LONG AFTER THEIR ATTEMPT ON ARNBJORN, THEY APPROACHED ONE OF THEIR SLAVES, A MAN CALLED EGIL THE STRONG WHO DESPERATELY WANTED TO BE FREE.
YOU CAN HAVE YOUR FREEDOM IF YOU MANAGE TO KILL BJORN, ARNBJORN, OR THORD.
I BET SNORRI WILL HAVE A PLAN.
IT WAS SAID THAT SNORRI'S PLAN WAS CUNNING, HOWEVER, EGIL WAS UNLUCKY IN HIS ATTEMPT.
trip
BJORN AND THORD FORCED EGIL TO TELL THEM EVERYTHING.
IT WAS THE THORBRANDSSONS!
AND THEN THEY KILLED HIM.

BACK THEN, ANYONE WHO KILLED ANOTHER MAN'S SLAVE WOULD HAVE TO PAY THE OWNER 12 OUNCES OF SILVER AS COMPENSATION WITHIN THREE DAYS OF THE KILLING.
THE THORBRANDSSONS WILL WANT COMPENSATION FOR THAT MAN.
THE BREIDAVIK BROTHERS AND THE THORLASKSSONS GATHERED A FORCE OF 60 MEN.
YOU'RE MAKING A MISTAKE. THIS MANY MEN WILL PROVOKE A FIGHT.
STAY BEHIND WITH YOUR BROTHER AND TWENTY MEN.
IF WE DO MEET AGAIN, STEINTHOR, I PREDICT YOU'LL TELL ME THAT YOU DIDN'T HAVE ENOUGH MEN.
MEANWHILE, SNORRI GOÐI MADE HIS MOVE TO GREET THEM.
IF THE THORLAKSSONS ACCEPT COMPENSATION AND HONOR THE TRUCE, THERE WILL BE NO BLOODSHED.
AWW!
SNORRI GATHERED HIS FORCES WITHIN THE THORBRANDSSON'S HALL AND WAITED FOR STEINTHOR TO ARRIVE WITH THORD BLIG.
NOBODY MAKE A MOVE. WE ARE NOT HERE TO FIGHT IF WE CAN HELP IT.
LET ALL WHO ARE HERE WITNESS THIS AS PAYMENT FOR THE LIFE OF THE SLAVE CALLED EGIL THE STRONG!

STEINTHOR INTENDED TO GO HOME AFTER THIS. BUT THORLEIF KIMBI PREVENTED THAT.
STOP THIS! WE HAVE A SWORN TRUCE! STEINTHOR HAS PAID THE PRICE FOR EGIL! LET THEM GO!
WHO DID THIS, MY SON?
STEINTHOR OF EYR.
SO MUCH FOR THAT TRUCE.
THUS BEGAN THE BATTLE OF ALFTAFJORD.
YOU'RE ON THE WRONG SIDE, STYR! STEINTHOR NEARLY KILLED YOUR GRANDSON.
THAT'S MORE LIKE IT, KINSMAN.
SOON A BAND OF 30 MEN ARRIVED TO INTERVENE AND STOP THE FIGHTING.
SNORRI AGREED TO STOP IF STEINTHOR WOULD ACCEPT A PERMANENT TRUCE.

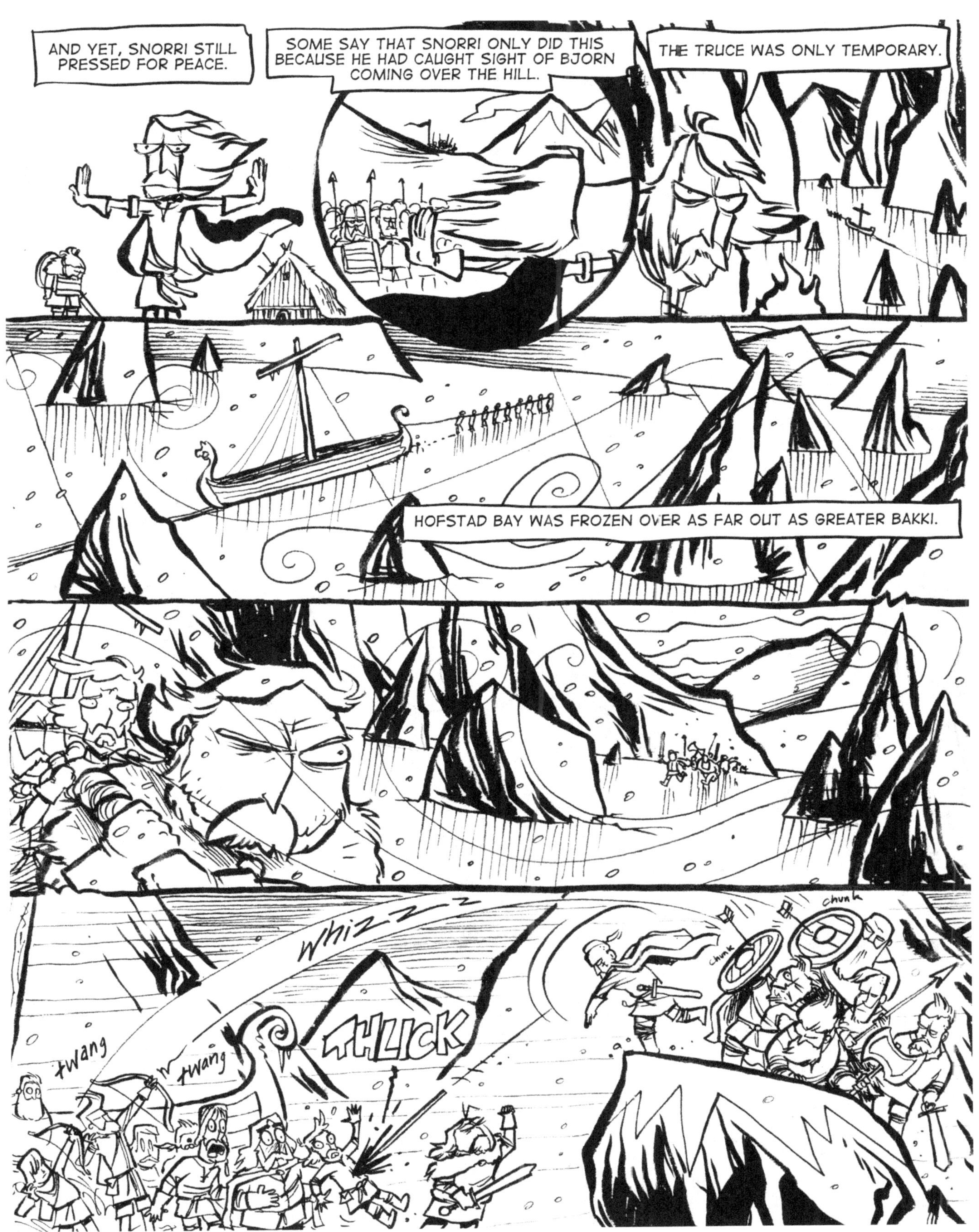
AND YET, SNORRI STILL PRESSED FOR PEACE.
SOME SAY THAT SNORRI ONLY DID THIS BECAUSE HE HAD CAUGHT SIGHT OF BJORN COMING OVER THE HILL.
THE TRUCE WAS ONLY TEMPORARY.
HOFSTAD BAY WAS FROZEN OVER AS FAR OUT AS GREATER BAKKI.
WHIZZZ
chunk
chunk
THLICK
twang
twang

THWAK
LOP
GRRR
WHIZZZ
LET'S TAKE THEIR HEADS, STEINTHOR!
I WON'T HARM A MAN ON HIS BACK, BROTHER.
SNORRI GOÐI HEARD ABOUT THE BATTLE OF VIGRAFJORD AND RUSHED TO THE SCENE, BUT HE WAS TOO LATE.

BACK AT HELGAFELL, SNORRI DID HIS BEST TO NURSE ALL OF THE THORBRANDSSONS BACK TO HEALTH.
IN SPRING, VERMUND THE SLENDER ARBITRATED A SUCCESSFUL SETTLEMENT BETWEEN THE TWO PARTIES.
BUT SNORRI'S TROUBLES WEREN'T OVER JUST YET.
YOU'VE GOT TO DO SOMETHING ABOUT BJORN!
SNORRI RODE OUT TO SETTLE THE MATTER ONCE AND FOR ALL.
SNORRI! JUST PASSING BY, OR DID YOU COME HERE WITH A PURPOSE?
WELL, THINGS MAY HAVE TURNED OUT A BIT DIFFERENTLY THAN I HAD HOPED.
YOU'LL ESCAPE WITH YOUR LIFE THIS TIME, BJORN. BUT PLEASE, STOP MESSING AROUND WITH MY SISTER, THURID. WE'LL NEVER HAVE PEACE UNTIL YOU DO.
EASIER SAID THAN DONE. I CAN'T RESIST HER WHILE I'M SO CLOSE.
THEN WHY NOT PUT SOME DISTANCE BETWEEN YOU TWO?
WHAT'S KEEPING A BOLD MAN LIKE YOURSELF HERE ON A FARM?
YOU'RE RIGHT, SNORRI. I'VE BEEN HERE FOR TOO LONG!
AND SO, THE MATTER WAS SETTLED. BJORN LEFT ICELAND SHORTLY AFTER. HIS SHIP WAS CAUGHT IN A STORM AND NO ONE KNEW WHAT BECAME OF HIM.

THIS BRINGS US TO THE YEAR 1000. UP UNTIL NOW ICELAND WAS PAGAN, BUT ALL THAT WAS ABOUT TO CHANGE WHEN GIZUR THE WHITE AND HJALTI ARRIVED FROM NORWAY TO PREACH THE NEW FAITH AT THE ALTHING.
FREYA'S A BITCH AND ODIN IS A DOG!
A VOLCANO JUST ERUPTED AND THE LAVA IS ABOUT TO SWALLOW MY PROPERTY. SURELY THIS IS A SIGN THAT THE GODS ARE ANGRY!
THE GROUND YOU ARE STANDING ON AND ALL THAT YOU CAN SEE WAS ONCE BURNING LAVA.
WERE THE GODS ANGRY THEN?
WE CANNOT LIVE DIVIDED BETWEEN TWO LAWS, CHRISTIAN AND PAGAN. WILL YOU ALLOW ME, THE LAWSPEAKER TO DECIDE?
AND SO, THORGEIR THORKELSSON HID HIMSELF UNDER A FUR BLANKET FOR A DAY AND A NIGHT TO THINK ON THE MATTER.
FINALLY, HE EMERGED WITH A SOLUTION.
WE MUST LIVE UNITED UNDER ONE LAW.
IF WE TEAR APART THE LAW, WE TEAR APART THE PEACE.
THAT'S HOW CHRISTIANITY WAS ADOPTED BY LAW IN ICELAND.
SNORRI GOÐI DID MORE THAN ANYONE ELSE TO SPREAD THE NEW FAITH TO THE WESTFJORDS.
Priests Wanted

THAT SUMMER, A SHIP ARRIVED FROM DUBLIN. ON BOARD WAS A WOMAN CALLED THORGUNNA FROM THE HEBRIDES.
SHE'S GOT A LOT OF FINE LINENS. STUFF YOU DON'T SEE HERE MUCH.
I HAVE NOTHING FOR SALE.
SNATCH
BUT THURID WASN'T GOING TO GIVE UP THAT EASILY.
YOU MUST COME AND STAY WITH ME AND THORODD.
I WON'T PAY YOU ANYTHING, OF COURSE. I AM STILL STRONG ENOUGH TO WORK FOR MY BOARD AND LODGING.
THORGUNNA WAS GIVEN A BED IN THE INNER CHAMBER.
ENGLISH LINENS! HOW MUCH FOR THE WHOLE SET?
I'M NOT GOING TO SLEEP ON BARE STRAW JUST TO SATISFY YOUR LUST FOR FINERY.
THORGUNNA WORKED HARD EVERY DAY.

ONE DAY A DARK CLOUD MOVED IN AS THEY WERE DRYING THE HAY.
WE SHOULD STACK THE HAY AND GET INSIDE.
BUT THORGUNNA REFUSED TO LISTEN.
THE STORM BURST, DRENCHING EVERYTHING.
BLOOD RAIN. THIS IS A BAD OMEN.
WHEN SHE DIDN'T ATTEND MASS THE NEXT MORNING, THORODD WENT TO CHECK ON HER.
PROMISE ME THAT YOU'LL BURY MY BODY AT SKALHOLT WHERE PRIESTS CAN SING MASS FOR ME.
I PROMISE, THORGUNNA.
YOU AND THURID CAN HAVE WHAT YOU WANT OF MY THINGS...
BUT YOU MUST BURN THIS BED AND ALL THESE LINENS TO ASHES. THIS IS IMPORTANT. I DON'T WANT TO BE RESPONSIBLE FOR WHAT MIGHT HAPPEN IF YOU DON'T DO THIS.
THORGUNNA DIED A FEW DAYS LATER.
YOU'RE NOT GOING TO BURN THOSE VALUABLE LINENS!
THORODD TRIED TO KEEP HIS WORD, BUT THURID GOT HER WAY.

SWISH
THE JOURNEY TO SKALHOLT WASN'T EASY FOR THORODD.
SPLORT
THEY FOUND A FARM IN STAFHOLTSTUNGUR AND SOUGHT SHELTER FROM THE STORM.
I'M SORRY. WE'VE GOT NO FOOD FOR YOU HERE.
IF IT'S ALL THE SAME TO YOU, WE'LL SPEND THE NIGHT HERE, EVEN IF YOU WON'T OFFER ANY FOOD.
Z
Z
Z
SCUTTLE

I DON'T THINK THORGUNNA APPRECIATED YOUR BRAND OF HOSPITALITY.
YOU ARE WELCOME TO EAT. TAKE ANYTHING YOU NEED. HAHA.
WORD OF THIS STRANGE EVENT SPREAD QUICKLY AND THORODD HAD NO TROUBLE FINDING HOSPITALITY ON HIS WAY TO SKALHOLT.
THE JOURNEY BACK WAS UNEVENTFUL FOR THORODD.
WITH THORGUNNA SAFELY IN THE GROUND, THE PEOPLE OF FRODRIVER THOUGHT THEIR TROUBLES WERE OVER.
THEY WERE WRONG.
WHAT IS IT?
IT'S A FATAL MOON.
THERE WILL BE DEATHS HERE.
THE STRANGE MOON APPEARED EVERY NIGHT FOR A WHOLE WEEK. AND THEN THINGS GOT WEIRD.

THE HAUNTINGS OF FRODRIVER BEGAN WITH THE SUDDEN DEATH OF A SHEPHERD.
THE SHEPHERD WAS NOT IN THE GROUND LONG.
!
THORIR SURVIVED THE ATTACK, BUT HE BECAME TERRIBLY SICK SOON AFTER.
AND THEN HE DIED.
AFTER THAT, BOTH THE SHEPHERD AND THORIR COULD BE SEEN WANDERING THE FARM AT NIGHT.
SOON SIX OTHERS WERE DEAD.
THAT'S WHEN THINGS GOT REALLY WEIRD.
scratch
scratch
scratch
ONE NIGHT, WHEN THORODD WAS OUT AT NESS FETCHING DRIED FISH, A STRANGE APPARITION ROSE UP THROUGH THE LIVING ROOM FLOOR.

THEY TRIED TO FORCE IT BACK INTO THE GROUND.
BONK
BUT NOTHING WORKED.
UNTIL YOUNG KJARTAN TRIED HIS HAND AT GHOST-SEAL SMASHING.
!
BONK!
THE NEXT MORNING, THORODD'S BOAT WAS FOUND. BOTH THE BOAT AND THE DRIED FISH WERE THERE, BUT THORODD AND THE CREW HAD DROWNED OFF THE COAST.
?
THURID AND KJARTAN HELD A FUNERAL FEAST FOR THE DROWNED MEN. WHEN ALL THE GUESTS WERE SEATED, THORODD AND HIS CREW SUDDENLY ARRIVED.
THIS IS GOOD. IT MEANS THAT THE SEA-GODDESS RECEIVED THEM WELL.
THE SAME THING HAPPENED THE NEXT NIGHT. AND THE NEXT.

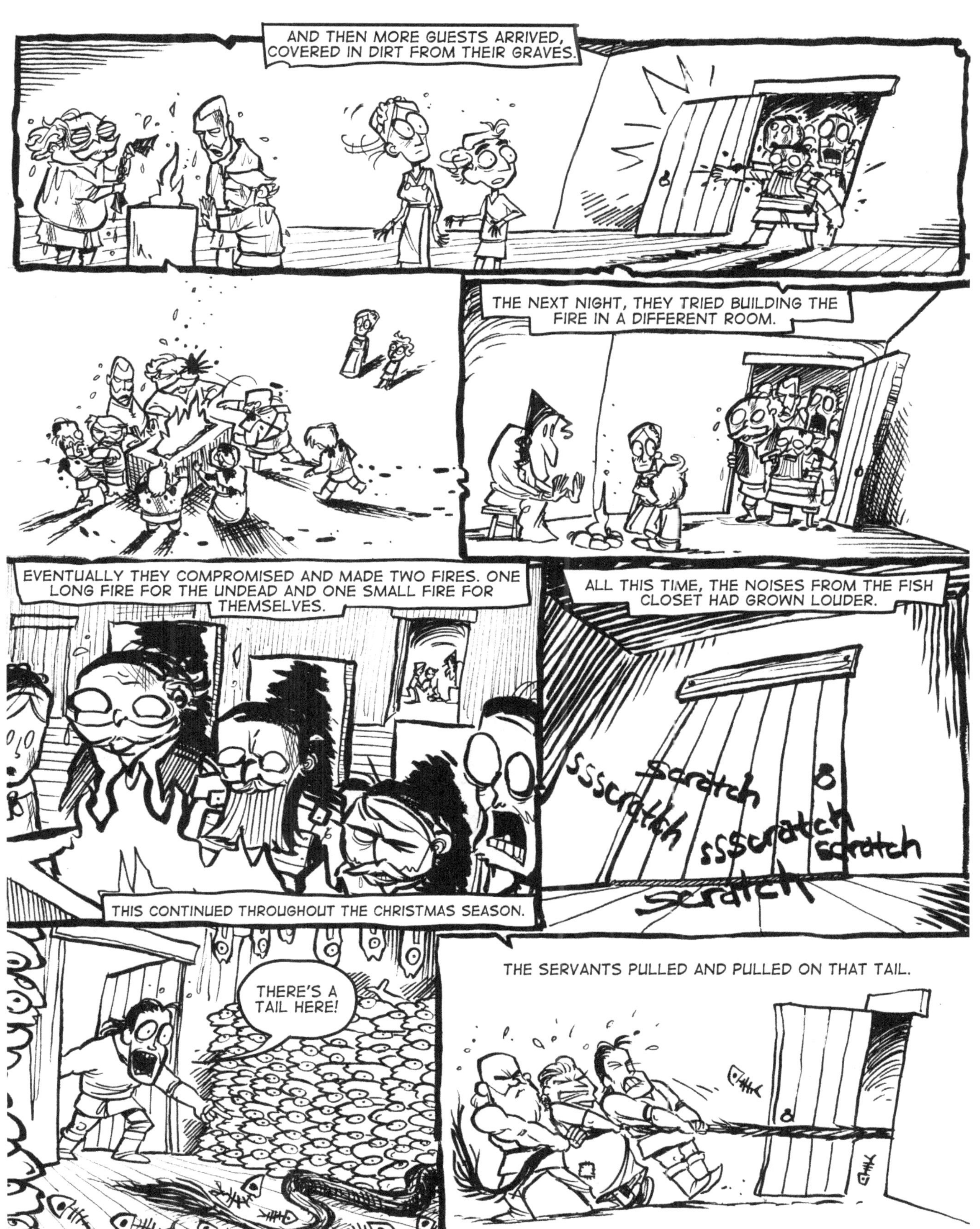
AND THEN MORE GUESTS ARRIVED, COVERED IN DIRT FROM THEIR GRAVES.
THE NEXT NIGHT, THEY TRIED BUILDING THE FIRE IN A DIFFERENT ROOM.
EVENTUALLY THEY COMPROMISED AND MADE TWO FIRES. ONE LONG FIRE FOR THE UNDEAD AND ONE SMALL FIRE FOR THEMSELVES.
THIS CONTINUED THROUGHOUT THE CHRISTMAS SEASON.
ALL THIS TIME, THE NOISES FROM THE FISH CLOSET HAD GROWN LOUDER.
sssscratch
scratch
sssscratch
scratch
scratch
THERE'S A TAIL HERE!
THE SERVANTS PULLED AND PULLED ON THAT TAIL.

WHATEVER IT WAS, IT NEVER CAME BACK.
ZIP
SOON AFTER THIS, THORGRIMA WITCH-FACE DIED. IN THE EVENINGS, SHE WAS SEEN WALKING WITH HER HUSBAND.
WHEN NEARLY EVERY SERVANT ON THE FARM HAD DIED, KJARTAN FINALLY RAN TO HELGAFELL TO SPEAK WITH HIS UNCLE SNORRI.
I HAVE A PLAN.
SNORRI SENT KJARTAN HOME WITH HIS SON, THORD THE CAT, AND A PRIEST.
THEN THEY HELD A DOOR-COURT.
I HEREBY SUMMONS THORIR WOOD-LEG FOR TRESPASSING!
I HEREBY SUMMONS THORODD TRIBUTE-TRADER FOR TRESPASSING!
ONE AFTER ANOTHER, THEY WERE ALL SUMMONSED AND SENTENCED.
YOU ARE BANISHED FROM THIS PLACE!
WE STAYED AS LONG AS YOU WOULD LET US.
I THINK IT'S TIME WE LEAVE.
AND SO, THE HAUNTINGS CAME TO AN END. AND KJARTAN TOOK OVER THE HOUSEHOLD AT FRODRIVER.

EVER SINCE ARNKEL'S DEATH, THOROLF TWIST-FOOT'S GHOST CONTINUED TO HAUNT THE REGION UNTIL MOST OF THE FARMS WERE LEFT ABANDONED.
THE FARMER RAN STRAIGHT TO THORODD THORBRANDSSON, HIS LANDLORD, FOR HELP.
THORODD RODE OUT TO TWIST-FOOT'S KNOLL AND OPENED THE MOUND.
THEY DRAGGED THOROLF'S BODY DOWN TO THE FORESHORE AND BURNT IT ON A HUGE PYRE.
THORODD TRIED HIS BEST TO GATHER THOROLF'S ASHES AND THROW THEM INTO THE SEA.
AFTERWARDS, FISHERMEN SAID THEY OFTEN SAW A STRANGE BULL WANDERING NEAR THE SHORE.
IN SPRING, THORODD'S COW GAVE BIRTH TO A FINE HEIFER AND A STRANGE, DAPPLE-GREY BULL.
THIS IS A FINE BULL!
THAT CREATURE ISN'T NATURAL. WE'LL ALL SUFFER IF YOU LET IT LIVE.
BUT THORODD COULDN'T BRING HIMSELF TO KILL THE YOUNG BULL.

THE BULL GREW QUICKLY. SOON HE HAD MAGNIFICENT HORNS AND A TERRIFYING BELLOW. THORODD CALLED HIM GAESIR.
DON'T WORRY. WE'LL KILL HIM IN AUTUMN AFTER HE'S FATTENED UP.
THAT'LL BE TOO LATE.
LATER THAT SUMMER, GLæSIR WENT WILD AND STARTED ATTACKING THE HAY BALES.
THORODD TRIED TO CONTROL GLAESIR.
!
THORODD'S MEN CHASED GAESIR ALL THE WAY TO A BOGGY AREA NEAR HELLUR, WHERE HE SUNK.
AND WITH THAT HAUNTINGS AND STRANGE EVENTS FINALLY CAME TO AN END.
MEANWHILE, FAR FAR FROM ICELAND, A TRAVELER NAMED GUDLEIF WAS BLOWN OFF COURSE ON HIS WAY HOME FROM IRELAND.
CéAD MILE FáILTE
!
!
THINGS GOT UGLY QUICKLY.

GUDLEIF AND HIS CREW WERE SPARED BY THE TRIBE'S CHIEFTAIN.

IS THAT GUY AN ICELANDER?

THE CHIEFTAIN SET GUDLEIF FREE AND SENT HIM HOME TO ICELAND WITH THE CONDITION THAT HE DELIVER A GIFT TO A FARMER AT FRODRIVER.

WHO SENT THESE GIFTS?

A MAN WHO IS A CLOSER FRIEND TO THE LADY OF FRODRIVER THAN TO HER BROTHER THE GOðI AT HELGAFELL.

AS THE YEARS PASSED, SNORRI GODI BECAME ONE OF THE MOST POWERFUL MEN IN ICELAND. PEOPLE ALWAYS TURNED TO SNORRI WHEN THEY NEEDED HELP.

SNORRI GOðI DIED AT TONGUE IN SAELINGSDALE A YEAR AFTER THE BATTLE OF STIKLESTAD. HE WAS BURIED AT THE CHURCH THAT HE HAD BUILT HIMSELF.

A GREAT MANY PEOPLE ARE DESCENDED FROM THE PEOPLE OF EYR. THE BEST OF THEM CAN TRACE THEIR LINEAGE BACK TO SNORRI GOðI.

www.ingramcontent.com/pod-product-compliance
Lightning Source LLC
Chambersburg PA
CBHW081140300726
48982CB00006B/1021

* 9 7 8 1 9 8 8 0 5 1 2 8 4 *